Alice's The Brady Bunch Movie™ Scrapbook

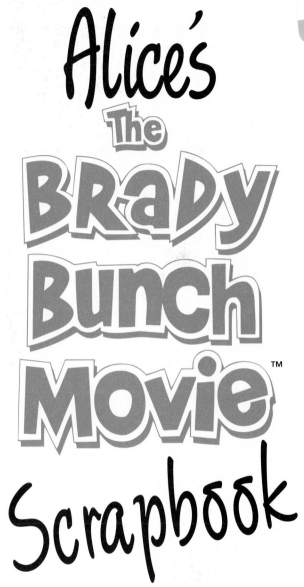

by Nancy Krulik, Ellen Stamper, and Madeline Wolf

SCHOLASTIC INC.

New York   Toronto   London   Auckland   Sydney

ISBN 0-590-67156-1
ISBN 0-590-73929-8 (Funtastic)

TM & © 1995 Paramount Pictures.
All rights reserved. Published by Scholastic Inc.

12 11 10 9 8 7 6 5 4 3 2 1   5 6 7 8 9/9 0/0

Printed in the U.S.A.   09

First Scholastic printing, September 1995

I've been working for Mr. Brady ever since the boys were little. I was there when Mr. Brady met the future Mrs. Brady. I was there when Greg, Peter, and Bobby met Marcia, Jan, and Cindy. And I was there when the kids had their first fight over the bathroom! To me, the Bradys are more than just the people I work for. They're my family!

Working for the Bradys sure keeps me hopping! There's nothing that the Bradys like better than a good potato-sack race!

Yep, we're all just one big happy family, living in a house Mr.Brady designed himself. I guess we thought we'd be living there forever, until the day our neighbor, Mr. Dittmeyer, decided to buy all the houses in the neighborhood and sell the land. Mr. Brady didn't want to sell.

It didn't seem like a big deal— until Mr. Brady got a letter from the government. He owed them twenty thousand dollars in back taxes! Ouch! If he didn't pay it, the government would take the house.

Either way, our house was in trouble!

Mr. and Mrs. Brady
were worried.
But they were
determined not to
let the kids know.

8

But have you ever tried to keep a secret in a house with six kids? (Especially when one of them is Cindy.)

Cindy has a slight problem. She's a bit of a tattletale. So naturally she tattled about her parents to her brothers and sisters. Oops!

Everyone had an idea on how to raise the $20,000...
Cindy wanted to sell lemonade.

Greg thought about getting a job as a rock star and tested out the idea on Cindy. Jan had the best idea of all. She thought the kids should enter a talent contest! But nobody ever listens to the middle child. I should know—I'm a middle child myself!

13

Marcia's To Do List

1. Doug/Charlie problem

2. $20,000 problem

3. Davy Jones problem

4. Brushing my hair

Marcia had a few problems of her own to solve first. There were the two boys whom she'd promised to go to the dance with, the famous singer who hadn't answered her letters, and, worst of all, it was a bad hair day!

When the going gets tough, Marcia Brady brushes her hair! There's no such thing as being too well-groomed.

Sell health
food products?
Marcia has a better
sales personality.

Since no one liked her talent contest idea, Jan had
to think of another way to raise money. But Jan
doesn't have much confidence.

17

Marcia and Jan thought they'd try modeling.

Poor Jan! Marcia was better at <u>that</u>, too!

Greg met up with a big-time music producer.
But Greg Brady didn't sound like a rock star's
name. Johnny Bravo did, though!

Time was running out, and the kids still hadn't raised the $20,000. Worse yet, Marcia still hadn't heard from her idol, singer Davy Jones. Meeting him would be a dream come true.

Mr. Dittmeyer was losing his patience with Mr. Brady. He really needed the Brady house to finish his land deal. And he was willing to do anything to get it. ANYTHING.

To the Bradys, this meant war. But even in the face of war, Mrs. Brady was well-dressed.

Mr. Brady tried to dress well, too…I've never had the heart to tell him that his pants, jacket, shirt, and tie don't ever seem to match.

23

The Brady kids were starting to show signs of stress. Everyone had some advice for them. And the advice came from some people who really knew what they were talking about!

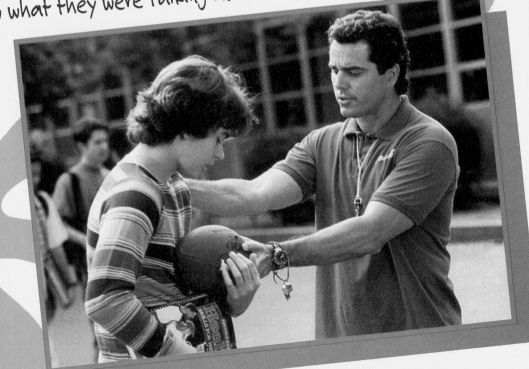

I had to keep my spirits up, too. I had always hoped that my boyfriend, Sam the butcher, would pop the question. But "Do you wanna go to the Meat Cutter's Ball?" wasn't the question I had in mind.

Still, life went on in the Brady household...
usually in the kitchen!

Jan still hadn't given up on her idea to enter the talent contest. This time, everyone thought it was a great idea. Unfortunately, they thought the idea was Marcia's!

The Brady Bunch was a hit!

PETER TORK   MICKY DOLENZ   DAVY JONES

The judges loved them. Marcia loved that one of the judges was Davy Jones! And Jan loved that the other kids finally remembered that entering the talent contest had been _her_ idea!

And Greg was finally a rock star—even if he wasn't Johnny Bravo anymore!

The house was saved!
And so was the neighborhood. Without the Brady house,
Mr. Dittmeyer's deal fell through.

What a groovy ending!